Veiled Reveries

Prose & Poetry

Jackie Lyn Paula Catipon

Ukiyoto Publishing

All global publishing rights are held by

Ukiyoto Publishing

Published in 2024

Content Copyright © Jackie Lyn Paula Catipon

ISBN 9789367952528

All rights reserved.

No part of this publication may be reproduced, transmitted, or stored in a retrieval system, in any form by any means, electronic, mechanical, photocopying, recording or otherwise, without the prior permission of the publisher.

The moral rights of the author have been asserted.

This is a work of fiction. Names, characters, businesses, places, events, locales, and incidents are either the products of the author's imagination or used in a fictitious manner. Any resemblance to actual persons, living or dead, or actual events is purely coincidental.

This book is sold subject to the condition that it shall not by way of trade or otherwise, be lent, resold, hired out or otherwise circulated, without the publisher's prior consent, in any form of binding or cover other than that in which it is published.

www.ukiyoto.com

DEDICATION

for those who carry worlds within, unheard and unseen…

for those who choose solace…

for the warriors who choose to fight their own battles silently…

for those who find comfort in being alone,

keep believing that some things are better off unspoken.

ACKNOWLEDGEMENT

To my family for their unwavering support to every piece that I write. To my friends who never fail to appreciate my art.

To the poets who have come before me – may you always tickle my creativity to write more.

To my partner in life, Richard, I could never be the person that I am today without you.

To my readers, for joining this ride. May you all find your story in between these words and be reminded that you are not alone.

Special thanks to Ukiyoto Publishing.

Contents

| Mirrors Lie | 1
| Ghost That Linger | 2
| State of Benign Love | 3
| Ephemeral Footprints Fading | 4
| Through The Frozen Fog | 5
| Haunting Hymn | 6
| A Walk Through the Graveyard | 7
| Will Never Be Enough | 8
| Asylum | 9
| Lucid Dreams | 10
| Unsung Ballads | 11
| Echoes of The Past | 12
| Relentless Hourglass | 13
| Parallel Universe | 14
| Caffeinated | 15
| Home Is Where You Are | 16
| You Burned Her | 17
| Someday Your Heart Will Sing | 18
| A Poet's Sacrifice | 19
| Unfitting Rhyme | 20
| Frosted Flowers of January | 21
| Bloomed From The Ashes | 22

| Inhaling Nostalgia | 23
| Ruins of Hate | 25
| Inception | 26
| The Firefly | 27
| To Lose You (Will Be The End Of Me) | 28
| An Ode to Myself | 29
| To The Stars Who Listen | 30
| Beneath The Harvest Moon | 31
| Labeled Poison | 32
| A Warrior and A Damsel | 33
| Bridges Burning | 34
| The Quest | 36
| The Burned Pages | 37
| Too Enough | 39
| Tranquility in Chaos | 40
| Seasons | 41
| He Only Gives Me Coffee | 42
| Why The Sky Cries | 43
| Jocel and Cory | 44
| Fading Photographs | 45
| Lingering Pain | 46
| Why I Love You | 47
| Never Letting Go | 48
| Missing Everything | 49

	Hypocrites and Bigots		50
	Sticking Around		51
	Forbidden		52
	Credence		53
	Found		54
	Solemn		55
	Dear September		56
	Coffee Break		57
	Mute		58
	Just for You		59
	Losing You		60
	Remembered		61
	Let Go		62
	Turnover		63
About the Author		64

I have been deceived
for as long as I can reckon,
even my eyes were fooled
that I choose not to look anymore;
I began to get scared
of what I would see
for all I know – from the very start
the woman that I see
is not me;
I have never hated anyone
more than I despise myself
because I am the wicked witch
that I never thought
I would ever become;
Mirrors lie —
for it tells me a different story…
How foolish of me to believe
that I was a beauty?
When I am a beast in a sheep's skin
in reality

| Mirror's Lie |

In an isolated place
in the universe
that I call home
I sip my afternoon coffee
with impractical thoughts running in my head;
What would I become
if I choose to stay?
Maybe, just maybe
still in the center of unrest…
What if I remain hidden?
No one will probably care…
I'll be like a ghost that linger everywhere—
like a train that got lost
in its tracks
and like a dreamer—
forever lost in reality;
A ghost that linger
and scaring no one – but me

| Ghost That Linger |

…to be embraced
by a securing, warm set of arms
that keep me safe
from my nightmares,
…to be kissed on the hand
in the middle of the night
when I fidget in anxiety
'till I calm down
…to be assured that there will be no heartbreaks
and only a heart
in the state of benign love—
that doesn't lie and greed;
It all feels genuine,
it truly exists,
and
it
is
staying…

| State of Benign Love |

The breeze outside is getting cold,
familiar ambiance is felt
but there's this change that
I cannot ignore—
the longing, the reminiscing—
of how the Holidays used to be
that I'd give my all to go back
to my Mom's special cooking,
to my Dad's gift-giving;
How innocence were the only thing
that mattered then—
and now replaced with so much guilt,
woes, and grief;
The ephemeral footprints
of the Holidays are now fading,
so as my childhood memories,
walking away towards a drastic path
of an unknown future,
leaving behind the cheers and music
from the Christmas morn—
embracing the truth
that the Holidays are not the same anymore

| Ephemeral Footprints Fading |

There are immeasurable times
that your love has saved me
from the edge of insanity—
even on times that
you drift off to sleep
long before me,
I find peace and serenity
knowing that you are already dreaming
into your own dreamland without me;
I shall be here when you awaken,
holding your hand and heart—
and never let go
even if I have to go
through the frozen fog, I would—
for all eternity—
until our next lives,
I surrender my love
for you, with you, alone
side by side, hand in hand

| Through The Frozen Fog |

They hear bells ringing,
carols and Christmas cheers—
but all I heed
are the old whispers
that bring me sorrows,
haunting hymns
that make me look back
from the past;
Haunting hymns
that even if I sing them smiling,
my heart cries in grief;
The songs that used to be
my childhood symbol of joy
now became like funeral songs
that would haunt me every year
to remind me how somber
everything is nowadays
that no celebrations can equal
or fill the void in me
that lingers still

| Haunting Hymn |

Gone are the days that
I used to wander off
the lavender fields—
or strolling through
the long lines of yellow tulips
in my favorite meadow;
Things have changed—
because all I know now
is a path towards an eerie forest
where crooked trees whisper
and critters crawl;
Everyday feels
like a walk through the graveyard
where silence and peace are at war,
where the residence crossed the light
we cannot see
I, maybe, in lined within this trail
for my feet always lead me here…anyway

| A Walk Through the Graveyard |

I always thought
that when I give my all
I'd receive the same…
until you said the best of your days
were not with me—
but with someone else
who weren't there for you
when you were at your most frail state—
when you hunger for almost anything—
when you gained something
in your end that made me proud,
I WAS THERE—
with you all the way
and it was all replaced
by just a few plates of provisions
that I, too, have been giving you everyday
Now I know—
that even if I give my soul—
and I'd still do it, nonetheless,
I will never,
EVER BE ENOUGH

| Will Never Be Enough |

I built my own prison
from all the hate words
that I've thrown myself
until they've become
indestructible fortress
and made escape impossible;
Now I am trapped
from the bars
that barricaded my freedom
to love myself
the way I should be!
I now hear echoes
from my everyday tears
that I conceal from everyone
for they will never understand
how cunning my mind is,
how it manipulates me
to have my own asylum
that will forever detain me
no matter how much I try
to break free

| Asylum |

Been tossing and turning
to capture the evasive sleep
that has been dodging me
for as long as I remember—
but when I succumb
to a slumber,
I start having visions
that make no sense at first
until it become almost real—
It's always about my fear
-the things that I dread
-or those that I repulse;
One thing is for sure—
I am starting to feel it again
where I can see what lies ahead;
These lucid dreams are my warnings—
and they are always peculiar and vile

| Lucid Dreams |

Here's to every word
that I choose not to speak—
for every piece of poetry
that I choose to conceal,
to all the feelings
I chose not to show;

I will always be at the corner
lurking away from the spotlight;
The darkness in me
could never stand anything bright;
I'll stay tranquil
for I've grown tired
being in a storm

All my unsung ballads
will forever be unknown

| Unsung Ballads |

As the year begins
and everyone seems to have
high hopes to what
life is about to offer,
I am here
with nothing but a wish
to finally silence
all the echoes of the past
that had been tormenting me
like nightmares that appear
even during daytime—
Echoes so deafening
that shatter my sanity beyond repair—
pleading to the skies
to finally set me free
and shit all the noises in my head
whispering, echoing,
"...*do it, do it*..."

| Echoes of The Past |

I watch in disbelief
how the sands of time
fall at the bottom
of this relentless hourglass—
to perhaps mock me
or even castigate me
for doing nothing but glare
to how much time has lost in me;
Dropping every grain
and no going back—
and one day
I'll walk away
from all the lost hours—
to create more moments
to be immortal and invisible—
to finally beat the time
and make it mine

| **Relentless Hourglass** |

If multiple reality does really exist, I hope my other self isn't scared of facing people. I hope she is brave enough to sing in the crowd – and if her voice quivers, she will belt out even more, and now so proudly that the crowd will cheer loudly. I hope she is always proud of herself and never doubts what she is capable of. I hope she isn't too broken that even on her usual days, she still feels beautiful no matter what. I hope she is living her dream – whatever it may be. I hope she found happiness and peace at a young age.

If a parallel universe truly exists, I wish to get a glimpse of her too – and I'll beamingly tell her, *"I'm happy that one of us made it, because I didn't."*

| Parallel Universe |

The bittersweet taste of coffee
used to rejuvenate me
from the days of exhaustion;
How the first sip
seems to awaken all my senses
to face the day
with enormous optimism;

But nowadays,
like my world seemed to tumble down,
when the bittersweet aroma
doesn't energize me anymore;
For it numbs me now—
so I could never feel anything
at least for a while;
So if you see me nonchalant—
I am caffeinated…
until I get back to my futile self again

| Caffeinated |

I have been searching for just a roof that would shield me from rain and hailstorms; and walls that would just protect me from cold winds and blowouts.

Gone to a desert that was so barren and almost incinerated me to death; with my feet burning, I reached an oasis that quenched my thirsts away – and I thought it would be all enough. Until you found me while I was wishing for a home – and not just a roof with walls, but a place where I am loved and protected.

It was you all along – the home that I needed – the home that I deserved. It is where you are, is my home where I am finally at my peace.

| Home Is Where You Are |

All the love notes you wrote for her—
-she kept them,
those flowers you bought and picked—
-she kept them,
those memories that you shared with her—
-she kept them;
Even those bruises that you caused—
-she kept them,
the scars from the cuts of your words—
-she kept them,
those early mornings that chose to ignore her—
-she accepted it,
those embers of hate that you gaslighted—
-it burned her
and left her scorched from within;
You used her,
you wrecked her…
and at the end,
you consumed her so much—
until she was left with nothing worth
keeping anymore

| You Burned Her |

From all those times you cried yourself to sleep, just to forget the pain for a while, someday you'll fall asleep in the arms of someone who made you smile the whole day;

From all your sacrifices that remained unseen by others, someday you'll reap all the blessings that you've shared – and it will be overflowing;

From all the punches and wounds that your heart has suffered from, someday your heart will sing and its melody will be heard as far as the mountain range ahead, and as high as the vast heavens…

| Someday Your Heart Will Sing |

I would always choose
the beauty of darkness
over the blinding light of the sun,
I would rather stay warm—
tucked in my sheets of paper,
scribbling the words I couldn't say aloud;
I would lurk in the corner
just to stay away from the clamor
and chaos of outside,
I would always choose to reach the stars
than to reach my destination
that doesn't exist,
I will write even while bleeding,
for it reminds me that I am alive

| A Poet's Sacrifice |

I'm always caught
in crossroads along the way;
Every turn and every step,
I had to make a choice—
to which aisle is to take
regardless of what awaits in the end;
A part of me chooses life—
to continue,
to keep on counting;
…while the other chooses death—
for it's just another path
to a destination unknown
but perhaps of a more comforting realm
than what life had promised;
No, maybe, I'd be lost for the meantime
because I am too tired
of taking the wrong road again—
just as writing a poetry
with an unfitting rhyme

| Unfitting Rhyme |

From the chilly breeze of autumn,
comes the stiff wind of winter
that makes her heart elated
because she can make more coffee
--so she can snuggle up alone,
free from the noises of yesterdays
that troubled her for weeks;
As she feels the warmth of her favorite potion
--she prays, grabs her pen,
starts scrawling across her mind
of the thoughts that haunt her
like frosted flowers of January
--unable to show her colors in full;
She asks the heavens above
to finally thaw the frigid air around her
--before her coffee gets cold,
to finally play on the snow
as her mind weakens for getting cold

| Frosted Flowers of January |

The earth beneath her shook tremulously,
spitted thunder and ashes simultaneously
where everything has gone gray
--dead are the colors
that once in flower beds lay

It took her time
It took her a while
Her roots were fragile

Until in the midst of the wasteland
she held up high,
she rises and broke the inevitable lie;
She bloomed from the ashes that used to bury her
and gave a hope of life
that no one else could muster;
She was red when everything was gray,
death was around her
but she refused to go
for there is strength and courage
from the beauty
that she, ever since, has and portray

| Bloomed From The Ashes |

I found myself lost again
in the middle of my evening coffee
lost in the thoughts
of how sacred childhood really is,
when I used to play pretend
like nothing else mattered;
Because when you it now,
they would think you're away with the fairies;
Those mornings that I looked forward to
were my rays of hope
--but the innocence in our laughter then
are now heard as noises;
As I ponder and observe
the last sip that I was about to take,
I breathed in its final aroma,
as if I was inhaling nostalgia
from the childhood that I'll never have again
--the childhood that my memory now holds
--and finally blinking to my reality
--getting up,
getting ready,
to face all uncertainties

| Inhaling Nostalgia |

Scattered debris,
suffocating dusts,
souls and the living scream in agony
for the death they never expected;
...and if they ever flee,
they'd be greeted by more explosions,
triggered and detonated by rage;
As the world watches, more children cower in fear
like rats being hunted by exterminators,
--clutching a dove of peace
that seemed to be flying away
from this piece of hell;
As we take sides, point which to blame,
more buildings collapse,
more houses turn into flames;
One day, we will face a child,
scrutinizing every rubble left behind,
rummaging concretes as graves,
we will all be stuttering to justify all the mess we've done,
all the ruins made by hate;
We will all be speechless,
as the innocence fades from his face
replaced by fear that we inflicted;
Now he watches, eyes full of hopelessness
confused and terrified of what he is seeing
--the playground that he used to run in the hours of late,
had turned into a wasteland,
into ruins of hate

| Ruins of Hate |

Non-stop inception
where nightmares spawn another terrors,
where we all just stare, petrified,
unable to move and act
to stop all the chaos
that shakes the very ground of Earth;
As more people succumb
to the fiery fury of other nations—
while some endure famine, infirmity, and abuse;

What have we become?
We are all in a deep slumber
where the world itself is a bad dream
where everyone of us are unable to wake up—
to do something,
to stand up for what is right,
to stand up for humanity once and for all;
But despite of everything, peace is still inevitable
if hate is left behind;
Explosions will become music,
hate will turn into love,
conspiracies will be unity
…and peace will finally stand tall

| Inception |

Your morning kisses
wake me up to a brand new day
with full of love and hope,
and your embrace
lullabies me to sleep—
giving me strength to face nightmares
that full me into downward slope;
In all my weaknesses,
you are my strength,
unknowingly, you have saved me
from countless deaths;
You are the firefly
that gave me light
when everything else around me
was darker than the darkest night

| The Firefly |

(piece is also available in Magkasintahan 3.0-Volume II)

No, I won't…
I won't even dare risk it…
It's like inflicting myself a wound
that will never heal,
a wound that will pinch my heart
until it beats no more;

To lose you, is to lose my being,
the last breath of air,
the end of my everything;
To lose you will be the end of me
as I have given you my future,
and I have surrendered my past…

You'll leave me in void
with nothing else to hold—
completely blind,
deaf,
and
mute

| To Lose You (Will Be The End Of Me) |

(piece is also available in Magkasintahan 3.0-Volume II)

I have never thought
that I'd be writing this myself—
for no one has written something for me—
might as well be inking
to remind me of me;
...of how I face every dreading day
with full of skepticism and fear
if I'll survive the next day;
...of how I continue all the words
that I need to say
despite the blockage in my brain;
Funny how I see myself as aa weakling
but my body and the universe is conspiring
to make me the warrior
that I truly am;

All I thought
I have been buried all along
with nothing more to do,
and yet here I am
about to break the earth for my reborn
...like a seed that sprouted strong roots
that will grow stems and branches
and eventually yield fruits
that will continue the legacy
that I thought I lost

| An Ode to Myself |

(piece is also available in Magkasintahan 3.0-Volume II)

With those times
that I looked up
to the heavens
with unseen clouds and nebulas,
I painfully plead
to the stars who listen
to my loudest whisper—
to my most silent reverie;

I lost count
of all the words I've spoken
to make me heard
across the universe;
I will now only seek the heaven's regard
…and to the stars who listen

| To The Stars Who Listen |

Months passed
since the last glimpse
of the only light
that I crave in the night—
the longing I have
from my anxious heart
is deep enough to hear
the echoes of my voice
when I scream so loud;

Up to the last minutes,
the clouds concealed it
just when I was about to break free—
from the chains of emptiness,
and now my yearning piles
as I continue to hype
in seeing it soon,
and the thoughts keep wandering more
beneath the Harvest Moon

| Beneath The Harvest Moon |

I'd take it everyday,
every waking days
for every dose of it
is an antidote
and every single drop
nurtures my dying heart;
It is addicting,
it makes me wanting more—
but if love could be a labeled poison
I would take it still—
I'd take the risk of dying
even with an enigmatic love
than to have nothing of it at all

| Labeled Poison |

I know I braved my journey to hell
and back again
in my solitary days
I fight my everyday foes
as treacherous as my mind,
I know I can move mountains,
I know I can slay dragons
that are on my way,
I know I am invincible; I know I am;

but

I crumble so easily in your arms,
like the petals of a dandelion
that were blown away by the wind
by just your touch;
I am a warrior alone
but a helpless damsel when with you—
it's almost impossible, but it's true;

So this is love as most people say—
So this is how it feels
to be loved,
so this is how it feels
when loved by you…

| A Warrior and A Damsel |

I hope someday you'll find the peace and love you've been chasing – at the wrong end.

I wish that somehow, you'll find the worth for all your efforts that were unmatched from the people you've bonded with.

I just hope that someday, may you not lose the ones who truly care for you genuinely – whom you chose to ignore because you were too busy giving them gold.

I sincerely hope that you'll finally prove me that you're doing the right thing this time,

as I burn the bridge between us – so I can never go back again.

| Bridges Burning |

I was hereby appointed
on a quest
where the journey is as hazy as the future,
with no clue what is about to come—
and I fled to accept my fate,
leaving the life full of hate;
As I commenced,
my footprints behind started fading;
With a thought of losing my path,
but continued nonetheless,
for I've been lost for so long anyways—
so I got more roads to take – but onwards;

There had been crossroads,
dead ends, and detours—
even points where I lost myself
       stumbled,
              crawled,
                      and got up again;
Faced the wildfire
that almost got me ashen,
my knees buckled in despair
for all the times I've fallen
from those traps and hypnotic words
Yet I stood still—
      bare,
           naked,
                empty…
But I'll get there
someday,
somehow—
to that haven
despite being still fogged out and hazy

| The Quest |

Flipping through the pages of my life's journal,
images of memories popping up
like fireworks in the night sky;
There had been blank pages
when I was literally empty inside and out
that no words came out of me;
There were scribbles floating,
hovering like a bird
that doesn't know where to go;

Then there are the buried pages
that no one else can read but me—
buried as deep as the trenches in the sea
that no one dared to explore and see,
the buried pages where I have written
while I was in the darkest cave,
and dug the earth to inhume every page,

the buried pages stayed there—
concealed and secured
ready to be written anew
with memories intact and captured

| The Burned Pages |

Looking back,
I thought we were too good to be true;
You were too good at least,
and I was too much of a coward,
a hopeless being
who just happened to love
every waking day;
Looking at us now—
maybe too redundant to our words;
but you are this everglow
who keeps on shining upon me
on my days of woes;
As I am always too much,
too afraid, too pessimistic,
too lonely—
but you are just enough—
always ahead of me
to cradle my gray clouds
before I start to rain,
Always on the calm side of the river
when I am in pain;
Could there be an exact word
to describe all of you?
No.
But I can proudly claim
that I'll never ever
ran out of words
to make more poetry
just for you

| **Too Enough** |

Silence always tortures me
for it always bring out
all the noises in my head
that feed on my peace;

How ironic
to feel tranquil
upon hearing chaos around me;
what a humongous change
to finally silence my loudest scream
by welcoming an unfamiliar clamor;

'tis the day
that I found tranquility in chaos
—at long last

| Tranquility in Chaos |

I grew up
in a tropical abode
with nothing but scorching sun
and torrential rain
where I either walk on the heat of the day
or swim against the current from flood and hurricane;

But when I sensed your presence in my realm,
you unleashed new seasons
that were too strange and new—
like a snowflake that clings
to a morning dew,
and a sparkle of dawn during noon;

Before then,
I used to slumber
with mediocrity and thwarting;
Now, as I close my eyes beside you
is like snowing
during an autumn night,
and waking up
to a clement winter morning

| Seasons |

I give him my trust
all in full
that I never had given before;

I give him all my love
after having been empty
and melancholy even more;

I give him my heart
after being shattered
in the most brutal way
that I thought I could never last
for one more day;

And he only gives me coffee—

They asked my why
as I turned my back to them
for they really don't know me that well,

Because for me, coffee is life
—and we both serve each other coffee
Every. Single. Day.

| He Only Gives Me Coffee |

The sky cries
in the midst of Summer Solstice
conquering its searing heat—
for days had been cruel
and the world is full of deceit;

The sky cries
but not enough to quench
the thirst of a barren land
that had been torpid
with nothing but a foul stench
from all the forsaken promises
and abandoned devoirs

The sky cries
—yet we still all wonder why

| Why The Sky Cries |

Looking back from our tender ages,
we were too carefree, euphoric
while we dance in the rain;
When days were light, nights were bright
and we ignored the noises of the world,
we went instead to the forest and explored;

We all had fights
but we have forgotten why
and ended being friends again
and never said our goodbyes;

Then came the aging,
had no idea of what was about to come,
we all eventually drifted apart,
still see each other once in a while,
in the street where we use to hang out all day;

But hey, Jocel and Cory,
Do you still know
when was the very last time
we went out to play and be kids?

| Jocel and Cory |

Found an old photograph
buried in a casket of my retrospect;
Squinted into a once with vibrant hues
to a now blurring sepia,
vague episodes filled my mind
of how everything used to be
—simpler, silent, happier
as I recognize the imprinted smiles
that are now growing dimmer too;

And as I look back,
it was a perfect moment captured
for it was the only proof
that there was a better life
that it is now
—immortalized and frozen
but vanishing away
and maybe in my memories too,
all photographs perhaps
are meant to fade away eventually
like the ones
that I have in my memory

| Fading Photographs |

For ages,
the pain still lingers
like a wound of yesterday;
From that day
of nothing but loss and despair
when I lost you
—like I lost my own life too,
with all those possibilities,
with all those imaginations
of "What if"
—all wasted to a nightmare
that forever won't go away;
But I'll endure
just like you want me too,
for the pain of losing you
still cuts me to the core of my being
is a proof of your existence
even just for while,
and a proof
that I am still alive and living

| Lingering Pain |

It wasn't just because
I found my peace in you,
nor I felt the warmth
that I've been longing for;

It wasn't just those efforts
that I discretely see,
nor those moments when I needed help
and you came and saved me;

It wasn't those times
when I needed shelter
that you promptly provided
when my world was too lopsided;

It really was
when I hated all myself—
when my world was all sorts of blue
—it was when you loved me
that made me love myself too

| Why I Love You |

In the midst of rain
and thunderstorms,
you go my back
and I got yours—
Through floods
and overwhelming convictions,
you held my hand,
calmed my senses
and took me over…
…and I'm never letting go

| Never Letting Go |

Just like how I make rhymes
to deliver my thoughts
and how I collect memories
in a pile of photographs,
I miss everything
—from the sunsets that I used to watch
to the rising of the moon
that are always hard to catch;

I miss everything
from all the books that I used to read,
to capture memoirs and people
—now turned to a dusty,
forgotten display
—on the same dusty shelf
where I also left myself
where I miss everything
that are now left somewhere
in the void

—lost,
and never to be found again

| Missing Everything |

Them—
who kneel with their eyes closed
near the pulpit
who also utter nothing but curses
and hate to others;

Them—
who speak about the Scripture and Gospels
also speak gossips about their neighbors;

Them—
who see the corruption of others,
also turn a blind eye
to their own mischievous deeds;

Them—
who declare to be righteous and good
are nothing but hypocrites and bigots
who spit venom,
think ill will,
and do deceits
So they can claim the throne
of which they thought is made up of gold—
but made up of rotting wastage
in all veracity

| Hypocrites and Bigots |

I have lost count
of the times
I told myself to leave
everything and everyone
for good;
My body is weak,
my mind is broken,
my soul is in pieces;
Every waking days
are challenges,
every sleeping hours
are tormenting—
but I still find myself
dreaming,
standing up,
fighting…
and at the end of the day
I stayed…
…and I am sticking around

| Sticking Around |

You wounded me
and even watched me bleed
with tears and crimson fluid
from my heart
and left me with nothing;

Therefore – in any way
you have no rights and audacity
to tell me
how to clean the mess you've made
how to silence my scream
and how to heal the wounds
that you've slitted

| Forbidden |

I held out my soul
and left it vulnerable
for you to protect
and to hold;
Only to find myself
in the middle of a courtroom
with an apple on my head
as you hold a bow and arrow
ready to fire

and I closed my eyes as I trusted you
to not volley at me

but you aimed it to my heart
and chose it to pierce and vanquish me

| Credence |

From all my birthdays I spent crying,
begging for a better life,
those days of nothing but anguish
that drowned and smothered me;
Those times that I lost myself
when I was trying to find someone
—only to be found by you,
whilst in my most unexpected time;

Everything got clearer,
everything got better,

I now celebrate my life
with full of hope,
and I began seeing the glimmer of light
that lead me
to a better hindsight

| Found |

It was when
I started shaking
as memories blinded my sight,
the fear, the pounding of my heart
against my chest,
and the coldness I felt
on that night
came crawling in my skin,
numbing everything I feel
once again;
As my tears fall silently
in the noises of the night,
I felt your arms secured me,
leering me away
from my fright;
You gently cradled me
with your embrace
until the chaos in me disappeared,
until I met my peace
once again
and slowly drifted me off to sleep;

I woke up
with a happy heart
knowing that you're
always there for me
to give me a brand-new start

| Solemn |

I may not have seen autumn
when leaves turn
into my favorite hues
when they fall down
from the branches that held them
to make way for a new beginning;

I wish to see it
and inhale its scent
down to my very soul,
but I'll settle
with your cooling breeze
brought by the rain and clouds
that seem to water me
and beckon the wind
to sing aloud;

Dear September,
You are the perfect month for me
for you signify courage
and change
to let go of has been
and welcome
a new beginning

| Dear September |

I should be having coffee
to appreciate life,
to feel and understand
the enigma that surrounds me,
and to just sit and rest

but then I am sipping
my favorite potion
from a broken cup,
boiled from a pot
rusted by time
to wave down
my anxious mind
from all the whispers
that warps my judgement

I should be having a coffee break
but I am the one breaking

| Coffee Break |

Loads of times
that I've chosen to cower
in fear
in the corner
when they ask me to speak;
There had been
sick moments
that I'd rather sew my mouth shut
than to utter words
I wanted to say;

Perhaps I am a mute
for I have been screaming
all my life—
so loud
that I lost all my voice
…except the ones
Inside my head

| Mute |

I just knew in my heart
that when it comes to you
I have a million things to say
—about how you
make my gloomy day bright
or how you treat me so right
—about how you suppress
the storm in my mind
or how you make me blind
on my insecurities,
my shortcomings,
my ghosts and demons;
But in the end,
I get lost in all those words
because I first knew
that no matter what I do
it will take a lifetime or two
but I would never run out of poetry
just for you

| Just For You |

Things haven't been the same
it even sound different
when I call your name;
My heart aches as
my hand shivers
when I bid goodbye
to your fading beauty
up in the sky;
I am losing you,
and I am letting you go
for I have been losing myself
as I walk away
from the one I have loved
for so long, for always;
Someday, I hope…
that I'll find the courage again
to look at you up there
and find myself once more
far from being insane

| Losing You |

How often do we reminisce
a memory – a moment
shared with someone special?
The calendar tells us only once—
How often do we give attention
to something as important as existing?
Our hearts tell everyday
but our minds, not too frequent—
At the end of the day
living or not,
we deserve to be valued,
we deserve to be given recognition,
we deserve to be noticed,
we deserve to be loved,
we deserved to be remembered…

| Remembered |

…to be wounded by someone
who should be healing you,
…to be hurt by someone
who should be taking care of you,
…to be crushed by someone
who should be lifting you up,
…to be abandoned by someone
who should be with for the rest of your life,

don't you think it is time
to let go of that someone
whom you are holding on for too long?

| Let Go |

Yes, you are still scared
of loud bangs in the kitchen
or of screams in your head,
you still have a list of your "what if's"
and long line of poetry to write,
you still long for rest and calm
and cry yourself to sleep
—you thought you're going nowhere
but take a look behind you
—you are still burdened by things,
yet this time
you don't wish to be gone
because all you want now
is to continue living…

| Turnover |

About the Author

Jackie Lyn Paula Catipon

As a mother of 4, Jackie officially became a published author in 2020. Since then, she has published 4 books in the next 4 years. She also co-authored 2 anthologies from Ukiyoto Publishing: "Magkasintahan 2.0 Volume I and Magkasintahan 3.0 Volume II).

From the humble town of Baler in the Province of Aurora, Jackie earned her degree in Bachelor of Arts in English at Mount Carmel College Baler and is currently working as a Technical Staff at TESDA Provincial Training Center – Baler. As a former Feature Editor in MCC Baler's Carmelian Faces, former Contributor Writer in TESDA Region I's Newsletter TESDA Chronicles, and a former SEO Writer, Jackie embraced her love for writing by being a part-time freelance Academic Writer and continuing her passion to produce more poetry books every year.

She also enjoys photography, being a mental health and animal welfare advocate. Coffee is her main potion. She is a proud Swiftie, a tattoo enthusiast, a Potterhead, and a good cook.

Milton Keynes UK
Ingram Content Group UK Ltd.
UKHW020354091224
451733UK00024B/71

9 789367 952528